THE
GHOST
COMES
CALLING

W9-BCO-015

Other Little Apple Paperbacks
you will enjoy:

Ghosts Don't Eat Potato Chips
by Debbie Dadey and Marcia Jones

The Haunting of Grade Three
by Grace Maccarone

No Such Thing as a Witch
by Ruth Chew

THE
GHOST
COMES
CALLING

BETTY
REN
WRIGHT

A
LITTLE APPLE
PAPERBACK

SCHOLASTIC INC.
New York Toronto London Auckland Sydney

If you purchased this book without a cover, you should be aware that this book is stolen property. It was reported as "unsold and destroyed" to the publisher, and neither the author nor the publisher has received any payment for this "stripped book."

No part of this publication may be reproduced in whole or in part, or stored in a retrieval system, or transmitted in any form or by any means, electronic, mechanical, photocopying, recording, or otherwise, without written permission of the publisher. For information regarding permission, write to Scholastic Inc., 555 Broadway, New York, NY 10012.

ISBN 0-590-47354-9

Copyright © 1994 by Betty Ren Wright.
All rights reserved. Published by Scholastic Inc.
APPLE PAPERBACKS is a registered trademark of Scholastic Inc.

12 11 10 9 8 7 6 5   5   8 9/9 0/0

Printed in the U.S.A.   40

For
Bob and Richard Swain,
who remember
Shaky Acres
and who loved it
as much as
I did

Contents

THE GHOST COMES CALLING

Chapter One

" . . . You'll Shake and Shudder Every Night."

When Chad Weldon stepped off the bus, he knew right away that something had happened in Bristol while he was away. For one thing, his father couldn't stop smiling. For another, his great-aunt Elsa couldn't stop frowning.

The smiles and frowns continued all the way home in the pickup, while Aunt Elsa asked a million questions about what was new at his cousin's house, and Chad's father chuckled at the answers. Scrunched between the grownups, Chad tried to figure out what was going on.

He noticed that they were talking only to him, not to each other. That meant the thing that had happened while he was gone was

1

pretty serious. His dad and Aunt Elsa argued a lot, but they hardly ever stopped talking to each other. The silence between them was scary.

That evening Aunt Elsa fixed chicken drumsticks and mashed potatoes, Chad's favorite dinner. It wasn't until they were through eating and the dishes were washed and they were sitting out on the front-porch steps that his father said, "Now, listen to this, boy. I've got a real surprise for you."

Chad could tell by the way Aunt Elsa sniffed that the surprise — whatever it was — was the reason for the smiles and the frowns and the not-talking.

"I sort of thought there was something," Chad said.

"Well, you bet there is!" his father exclaimed. "I've bought us a little place on Perch Lake, just about an hour from here. A log cabin! For weekends and vacations and just getting away. How about that?"

"A shack," Aunt Elsa said, staring out at the pansy bed. "He's bought a shack, and he's used every cent he had in the bank to pay for it."

"It was too cheap to pass up," his father went

on, as if Aunt Elsa hadn't spoken. "We're going to have us some great times out there."

Chad didn't know what to say. He was excited and scared at the same time. The money in the bank had been their nest egg, in case his father lost his job with the Bristol parks system. Knowing it was gone gave Chad a funny feeling in his stomach.

"I never thought we'd have a cabin," he said carefully, not looking at Aunt Elsa.

His father's smile grew bigger. "Didn't know it myself. I just happened to be down at the courthouse when they were selling it off. Pretty lucky, if you ask me."

"Pretty dumb, if you ask me," Aunt Elsa snapped. "All that money — for a shack in the woods!" She stood up suddenly and marched into the house. The screen door slammed behind her.

"Now, don't worry, she'll come around," Chad's father said after a minute. "She's put up with *us* ever since your mother died, and she'll get used to the cabin, too." He reached over and tapped Chad on the head. "Why don't you go across the street and tell Jeannie about the cabin?" he suggested. "I've been keeping it a secret till you got home. You know, her folks have a place at the other end of Perch Lake, so you kids will have a lot of fun together."

Chad wasn't in a big hurry to see Jeannie Nichols, but he went anyway. Jeannie was nearly two years older than he was, and if she was bossy, sometimes she was pretty smart, too. Maybe if he told her about the cabin, he'd feel better about it himself.

As it turned out, he felt worse. A lot worse.

"I know that falling-down old place!" Jeannie exclaimed, wrinkling her nose. "My dad said it was for sale, but he didn't think anyone would buy it. What a stitch!"

She always said "What a stitch!" when she thought something was really funny.

Chad felt his face redden. "I think it's great!" he said. "I can hardly wait to get out there."

Jeannie snickered. "Everybody at Perch Lake calls that place Shaky Acres," she said. "Guess why."

"I don't care why," Chad told her crossly. "It's a silly name. *We'll* never call it that."

"I'll tell you anyway," Jeannie said. "They call it Shaky Acres because the cabin's so run-down and because it's haunted, that's why."

Haunted! Chad stared at her.

"You didn't just buy a cabin, you bought a ghost," Jeannie went on. "And when you stay there you'll shake and shudder every night. What a stitch!"

Chapter Two

"Somebody's Coming!"

It was raining Saturday afternoon when they drove out to Perch Lake.

"One more curve and we're there," Mr. Weldon shouted. "Hang on!"

"One more b-b-bump and I'm going to be sick!" Aunt Elsa exclaimed. She had a hand on her gray curls, as if she were afraid her head might bounce right off.

Chad didn't mind the bumps. He stared into the woods that pressed close to the pickup. These were his very own woods. He could go exploring whenever he wished.

The road ended in a clearing. "Here it is!" Mr. Weldon said proudly. "That's our log cabin, boy. What do you think of it?"

Chad stared at the little log house in the middle of the clearing. "Wow," he said softly. "It's great!"

"Great!" Aunt Elsa snorted. She opened the truck door and slid to the ground. "Just look at how that roof sags. It could fall down on top of us."

Mr. Weldon just smiled. "But smell those logs," he said. "I love that smell!"

"So do I," Chad said. He tried not to listen to Aunt Elsa as she followed them into the cabin, complaining all the way.

"No electricity. No running water! And look at the gaps between some of these logs. A mouse or a bat could squeeze through, easy as anything."

Chad's father patted her shoulder. "It'll just take some getting used to," he said. "The gas stove works, there's a pump in the backyard, and there's an old iron stove for heat. We'll be fine."

He led them through the living-and-dining-room to a porch that stretched across the front of the cabin. Its windows were covered with rusty screens.

"Aunt Elsa can have the bedroom, and you

and I'll sleep out here, Chad," he said. "We can smell those night breezes and listen to the waves as we go to sleep."

"And get soaked when it rains," Aunt Elsa snapped. "Some fun!"

"We aren't staying here tonight." Mr. Weldon was beginning to sound a little annoyed. "And we can always set up our cots in the living room when the weather's bad. Cheer *up*, Aunt Elsa."

Chad looked out at the lake. A heavy gray mist covered most of it, but he could make out a little pier stretching over the water.

"I'm going out on our pier," he said. He liked saying "our pier."

"The rain — " Aunt Elsa began. She stopped when Chad's father gave her a look. "Well, don't blame me if you catch a beauty of a cold," she said and stomped back to the kitchen.

The pier was narrow and rickety. Here and there boards were missing, but Chad marched right out to the end. He sat down and dangled his feet over the edge, so his sneakers almost touched the water. The mist closed around him.

This is fun, he thought, but even as he thought it, he knew he wouldn't sit there very long. It was actually sort of scary — like drifting alone on a raft far from shore. The rain was gentle and warm, but he began to shiver, just a little.

They call it Shaky Acres, Jeannie had told him. What would she say if she were sitting here with him now?

A dog howled. It sounded as if it were out on the water, which was crazy, of course. Then Chad heard another noise — a soft *splish-splash*, like oars dipping into the water. *Must be waves*, he told himself, but when he looked down at the lake, it was as still as glass.

The sound grew louder. It *was* oars. It had to be. And they were coming closer. In a minute the boat would break through the mist and he would see —

Suddenly, Chad didn't want to see what was coming out of the mist. He scrambled to his feet and raced back along the pier, jumping over the open places. Up the path he hurtled to the cabin, almost bumping into his father as he burst through the porch door.

"Somebody's coming!" he gasped. "In a boat. I heard the oars."

Mr. Weldon looked at the lake. "Somebody's out in a boat in *that*?" he said. "No way, boy.

Your ears are playing tricks on you."

"There was a dog howling, too," Chad said stubbornly. "Wait a minute. You'll see."

They stood side by side, staring out at the mist. Pretty soon Aunt Elsa came to join them.

"This place gives me the creeps," she said, after one minute passed, then another, with nothing to look at but rain and fog. "You can't even see the neighbors' cottages."

"There aren't any neighbors," Mr. Weldon told her. He put one arm around her and the other around Chad. "That's why I know this young man's imagining things. There are no cottages and no dogs. It's a big lake, and there isn't another living soul at this end of it."

Chapter Three

On the Pier

Twice that week, Chad dreamed he was at the end of the pier at Perch Lake. He could hear the soft *splish-splash* of oars coming closer, but when he tried to run, he couldn't move. Each time he woke up yelling and scared.

"Think about something fun," his father suggested, the second time it happened. "Think about going swimming or fishing. Think about how great it will be to spend the whole weekend out at our cabin."

Chad didn't say anything.

"I bet he'd rather stay in town with his friends," said Aunt Elsa, who had been awakened by the noise. "Same as me."

"What were you dreaming about, anyway?" Mr. Weldon asked. But Chad wouldn't tell him.

The dreams were Jeannie Nichols' fault, really. If she hadn't talked about ghosts and haunting, he would have forgotten the strange sounds he'd heard at the end of the pier.

That week he used the back door and went down the alley so he wouldn't run into Jeannie and have to answer questions about the cabin. Then on Thursday his father spoiled everything by meeting Jeannie and her mother at the drugstore.

"Guess who's coming over from her cottage to spend Saturday at our place," he said when he came home. "You kids can go swimming together."

Chad groaned.

"I thought Jeannie was a good friend of yours," his father said, looking at him in surprise. "Are you mad at her, or what?"

"I'm not mad," Chad told him. "She just — she just talks too much." He picked up his basketball and hurried outside, so he wouldn't have to explain about Jeannie. She was fun to shoot baskets with, and she could run faster than anyone he knew. It was just that she thought she knew everything, and more often than not she said things that made Chad feel as if his insides were tied in knots.

That was it, he decided, as he crouched in front of the basketball hoop. Jeannie was okay, but she talked too much.

"My dad says your dad can't hang on to a nickel," Jeannie announced on Saturday afternoon. She was following Chad down to the pier in front of the cabin. Perch Lake sparkled in the sunshine, and all around them the pine trees smelled like Christmas.

"That's a lie," Chad said, even though he'd heard Aunt Elsa say the same thing many times. His father was like a kid, always ready to try something new. Like owning a lake cabin. But the cabin was going to work out fine, he told himself. They were lucky to have it, no matter what anybody said.

A couple of hours later he was sure he was right. The lake was cool and clear, and even Jeannie had to admit the sandy bottom around the pier was perfect. They took turns towing each other in the giant inner tube Jeannie had brought from her cottage at the other end of the lake, and they had dog-paddle races. They played water ball. When they were tired, they stretched out on the pier and let the sun dry them.

"This is neat," Chad murmured sleepily. He wondered how he could have been so frightened, just a week ago, in this very spot.

"It's pretty nice here," Jeannie admitted. "Maybe — " She sat up suddenly and stared into the woods. "What was that?"

"What was what?"

"I thought I heard a dog howling." She shivered and wrapped her towel around her shoulders. "My dad said Tim Tapper had a dog. It was big and black and it had sort of reddish eyes."

Chad refused to ask who Tim Tapper was. He was pretty sure he didn't want to know.

"Tim Tapper was the man who built your cabin," Jeannie told him, anyway. "He and his dog lived here at Shaky Acres for years and years."

"Don't call it that," Chad said. He squeezed his eyes shut, pretending to go to sleep, but Jeannie kept talking.

"Tim Tapper lived here until the day he drowned when he was out fishing. They think he must have fallen out of his boat. Nobody knew what had happened until they found his empty boat bumping up against the other shore — maybe weeks later."

Chad felt goosebumps pop on his arms, in spite of the sun. He sat up. "What happened to the dog?" he asked.

"Nobody ever saw it again," Jeannie whispered. She stared into the woods as if she expected to find reddish eyes glaring out at them. "He must have run off when Tim Tapper didn't come back. He probably died of a broken heart, poor thing."

A tiny puff of cloud drifted across the sun, darkening the water. Wind sighed through the branches of the pine trees.

"You're making up this stuff," Chad said crossly. "Somebody from Tim Tapper's family would have come looking for him when he didn't come back. They probably took the dog home with them."

Jeannie shook her head in her know-it-all way. "Tim Tapper didn't have a family. He didn't have one living soul but that dog. He was poor as a churchmouse and mean as a weasel. And they say he's been haunting Shaky Acres ever since."

A car horn blasted. The sound was so loud

and so unexpected that they both jumped.

"That's my mom come to pick me up," Jeannie guessed. She scrambled to her feet and ran along the pier. "See you tomorrow, maybe," she called. Then she stopped and grinned back at Chad. "Have a good night," she said, rolling her eyes. "If you can."

Chapter Four

The Ghost Comes Calling

That night Chad and his father played Scrabble after the supper dishes were done, and Aunt Elsa knitted.

"Nice soft light," Mr. Weldon commented, gesturing at the kerosene lamp in the middle of the table. "I feel like a pioneer, don't you?"

"Hmmf," Aunt Elsa sniffed, but she didn't sound especially unhappy.

"This is neat," Chad said. He loved the cozy cabin. If only he didn't have to keep checking the windows to see if there was anything looking in at them!

"Jeannie Nichols is a dope," he said. The words tumbled out before he could stop them.

The grown-ups looked at him in surprise.

"What a way to talk about that sweet little girl!" Aunt Elsa scolded. "I don't know what gets into you sometimes, Chad."

Soon afterward, she said good night and went into the tiny bedroom, pulling the burlap curtain across the doorway behind her. Chad and his dad went out on the screened-in porch to set up their cots.

"Maybe we should sleep inside," Chad said, staring out into the moonlight. "It might rain or something."

Mr. Weldon chuckled. "It's not going to rain, and it's not going to snow either," he said. "You're going to love sleeping out here, boy — you'll see."

He did like it, Chad had to admit, as long as his father was awake. The trees rustled outside the windows, and the lake made a soft lap-lapping sound. An owl hooted in the woods, and another owl answered.

"Smell that air," his father murmured sleepily. "You're going to remember this all your life, Chad." Then he began to snore.

Chad curled up into a ball. All at once the night seemed to close in around him, and even though his father was just a few feet away, he'd never felt so alone.

He tried closing his eyes, but they popped open right away. There were too many windows to watch. The friendly whisper of the trees began to sound like rustling footsteps, and the moonlight turned gray and eerie.

A dog howled.

For a moment Chad thought he had imagined the weird, far-off sound. Then he heard the howl again, much closer this time. He pulled his blanket over his head and moved one corner back just enough to peek out. There, peering in at him through the nearest window, was the face of a fierce old man. Deep-set eyes glared out of a white face, and a clawlike hand was spread against the screen.

"Dad!" Chad's terrified shout came right from his toes. His father shot up so fast, he almost fell off his cot.

"What? What?" he demanded. "What's wrong?"

Chad pointed at the window next to his bed. It was empty now, but he could see that furious white face as clearly as if it were still there.

"S-Someone's out there," he stammered. "An old man — I saw him!"

"What's happening?" Aunt Elsa cried from the doorway leading into the cabin. "Are there burglars?" She looked like a ghost herself, in her long white nightgown and white hair net.

Mr. Weldon pulled on trousers over his pajamas and scooped up the flashlight from the floor. "Stay here," he ordered. "I'll check around outside."

Chad sat shivering on the edge of his cot. Outside, the beam of the flashlight danced around in the dark, diving down below the windows and then pointing into the woods.

"We never should have come here," Aunt Elsa moaned. "I knew it in my bones."

"There was a dog, too," Chad called hoarsely out the window. "I heard it."

Aunt Elsa gasped. "A dog!" she exclaimed. "What would a dog be doing here? Unless it's a wild one, of course."

The flashlight beam disappeared around the back of the cabin and then returned. Mr. Weldon came back inside, shaking his head and limping.

"Stepped on a sharp twig or something," he explained. "But there's nothing out there, folks — no old man, no dog, no footprints. Nothing." He grinned at Aunt Elsa. "Chad's had another one of his bad dreams."

Aunt Elsa looked as if she didn't believe him. "Well, I won't sleep another wink," she said as she backed into the cabin living room. "And it wouldn't surprise me if there were prowlers," she muttered from the darkness. "Not one bit."

Chad waited till his father was back in bed. Then he tried to explain what he'd seen. "The man's face was white and shiny and awful," he whispered. "He didn't look real."

Mr. Weldon yawned. "You're right, boy — he wasn't real. It was all just a dream, and dreams can't hurt you. So go to sleep, and quit scaring your great-aunt out of her wits."

Chad lay down and pulled the covers back over his head. Carefully, he moved the sheet so that a little air could get in but he couldn't see out. He knew he wouldn't go to sleep — not for hours. Because now he knew what Tim Tapper looked like — and who could sleep

knowing someone like that might be just outside the window?

Shaky Acres is the right name for this place,
he thought miserably. *I'm going to be shaking
all night long.*

Chapter Five

A Mystery in the Woods

Chad was grateful that Sunday morning was gray and drizzly. The weather gave him an excuse to stay inside the cabin.

"I think I'll chop some wood," his father announced after breakfast. "We're going to need fuel for the stove when the evenings are cool. What are you going to do, boy?"

"Read my sports magazine," Chad said quickly. "For a while, anyway."

"You can bring in a couple of buckets of water for me first," Aunt Elsa said crisply. "And you can wipe the breakfast dishes, too. Wiping dishes is better than wandering around outside with who-knows-who sneaking through the woods."

Chad agreed with her, but he did his chores silently and just shrugged when she asked if he wouldn't rather be back in Bristol shooting baskets. What was the use of complaining? Shaky Acres belonged to them now. His father's cheerful whistle, as he chopped wood outside the kitchen window, told him that what had happened last night wasn't going to make any difference at all.

"I'll take a swim with you kids later on," Mr. Weldon announced at lunch. "The sun's coming out — did you notice?"

Chad had forgotten Jeannie might come back Sunday afternoon. He wondered what he'd say if she asked if he'd been nervous last night. It was hard to lie to Jeannie — she always seemed to see right through him — but he didn't want to tell her about the face in the window. She'd say "I told you so" and make things even worse than they were.

The way it turned out, he didn't have to tell her anything. He was lying on the pier when the Nichols' car drove into the backyard. Soon he heard Jeannie and his father coming down toward the lake together.

"Chad woke us up in the middle of the night,"

his father was saying in an offhand way. "He had a bad dream — thought he heard a prowler."

"No kidding!" Jeannie exclaimed. "I bet he really did hear someone. I bet he heard a ghost — "

"He's had a couple of nightmares at home, too," Chad's father went on, as if she hadn't spoken. "I've been wondering what could be bothering him."

"Well," Jeannie said, and stopped.

"Because if somebody's filling his head with a lot of dumb ideas, that person could be in big trouble. I'd probably have to talk to that person's parents."

"Oh." Chad could tell Jeannie didn't know what to say. "Lots of *little* kids have bad dreams," she murmured after a moment. Then he heard her run out on the pier. The big inner tube sailed over his head and hit the water with a *thwonk*.

"Come on, sleepyhead," Jeannie yelled. She grabbed his wrist and dragged him to his feet. "I'll pull you around in the tube first, okay?"

They both jumped off the end of the pier.

Chad went right to the bottom and opened his eyes so he could see where Jeannie was. Quickly, he grabbed her ankles and tipped her over backward. That would teach her to call him a little kid.

When they came up, sputtering, Chad's father was in the water, too, and was swimming away with the inner tube.

"Get him!" Chad shouted. For the next hour they paddled and ducked and splashed water at each other, till they were all waterlogged and shivering.

"I'm going in," Mr. Weldon said at last. "I need a lemonade break."

"I want to dry off in the sun," Jeannie said.

"Let's hike up the road," Chad suggested. He really didn't want to walk in the woods, but he didn't want to lie on the pier and answer questions, either. If they went exploring, Jeannie would have something else to think about besides what had caused Chad's latest "bad dream."

They draped their towels around their shoulders and set off on the winding road that led from the cabin to the highway. Chad walked in one rut, Jeannie in the other. Tiny frogs hopped away in front of them like popcorn popping from a pan.

"Where does that go?" Jeannie demanded suddenly. She was pointing at an even narrower trail that branched off from the one they were on.

"I don't know," Chad said. The little road was partly hidden by ferns and tall grass. He hadn't noticed it when they'd driven by in the pickup.

They stared into the shadowy opening for a moment, and then Jeannie started walking again. "Let's go out to the highway," she said impatiently. "Come on."

Chad felt suddenly daring. Maybe it was because he could tell Jeannie didn't like the looks of the mysterious little trail.

"We *know* what the highway looks like," he said. "I'd rather poke around in here. You don't have to come if you're afraid to."

"I'll come," Jeannie snapped.

There was nothing to do then but wade into the grass and plunge through the narrow opening. All at once, the rest of the world seemed far away. Sunlight touched only the top branches of the trees around them. Birds sang up there, but otherwise the woods were quiet. It was sort of spooky, Chad thought, but he wasn't really scared. He liked the tall trees and the good smell of growing things.

"You could get lost in here," Jeannie said in a low voice. She sounded as if she wanted to turn back, but Chad kept on walking.

The road curved and ended, unexpectedly, in a small clearing. Chad stopped so suddenly that Jeannie bumped into him.

"Look at that!" he exclaimed. "It's a truck!"

"An old, *old* truck," Jeannie added. "The weirdest old truck I ever saw in my entire life."

They moved closer for a better look. The truck had been red once, but the paint had faded, and the lettering on the sides was almost entirely worn off. The only windows were at the front and the back, but the glass was so dirty that they couldn't see inside.

"The tires are gone," Chad pointed out. "It's sitting here on its bare wheels."

Jeannie started to say something, stopped, and started again. "I bet this was Tim Tapper's truck," she whispered. "I bet this is what he used to drive into town for supplies."

Chad had been about to try the door on the passenger's side, but at the mention of Tim Tapper's name he stepped backward.

"You're scared," Jeannie said, sounding pleased. "Well, if you have another bad dream tonight, don't you dare blame me. And don't tell your father."

"You're scared, too," Chad retorted. She had a lot of nerve saying that, when she hadn't even wanted to explore the trail in the first place. He grabbed the rusty door handle and turned it. At first the door didn't move, but then it swung open with an eerie creak. He stepped up on the running board and peeked inside.

A blast of hot air hit him, and something small scurried under the driver's seat. The passenger seat had been taken out, so he could see all the way to the back of the truck.

"There's a long bench on each side," he reported. "People must have gone for rides in this thing."

Jeannie snorted. "Who'd want to do that?" she demanded. "What a stitch!"

BANG! BANG! BANG! The truck rocked under three heavy blows that echoed like gunshots in the silent woods. Chad leaped off the running board and hurtled across the clearing, with Jeannie right behind him. Down the trail they raced, expecting every minute that the thing — whatever it was that didn't want them in the clearing — was right on their heels.

Chapter Six

On the Magic Road

Aunt Elsa was in the backyard pumping water when Chad and Jeannie burst out of the woods. She looked up in alarm as they raced toward her.

"What's wrong?" she demanded. "You two are white as chalk!"

Chad opened his mouth to tell her what had happened, but then he remembered his father's warning: *Quit scaring your great-aunt out of her wits.* He picked up the two filled buckets and staggered toward the back porch. "We just felt like running," he said, panting.

"I'll open the door," Jeannie offered. She almost fell up the steps in her haste to be the first one inside. Aunt Elsa followed, shaking her head.

"Don't tell me then," she muttered. "But if you saw a prowler again, you'd better tell your father, Chad. He's down at the lakefront mending that slapdash pier."

"We didn't see anyone," Chad told her. That, at least, was the truth. "We found an old truck in the woods, though. It looks as if it's been there forever!"

"That's odd." Aunt Elsa sounded interested in spite of herself. "Now what in the world . . . " She seemed to be trying to remember something. Then she waved the thought away and opened the big cooler they'd brought from home. "How about some lemonade, you two? And maybe a pecan cookie or two."

Chad sighed with relief. No more questions! While Aunt Elsa poured the lemonade, he scowled warningly at Jeannie and put a finger to his lips. They sat at the round table, nibbling cookies and not looking at each other until a car drove into the backyard.

"That's my mom," Jeannie said. "I have to go." She thanked Aunt Elsa for the snack and hurried out without a backward glance.

After she'd left, Aunt Elsa produced a whole list of chores she'd been saving for Chad. Take the sheets off the cots. Sweep the porch. Stack the freshly cut wood next to the back porch. It was evening before he had a chance to talk to his father alone.

"Now I'm going to pack up the food we're taking home," Aunt Elsa announced after supper. "You two keep out from underfoot till I'm through in the kitchen."

Mr. Weldon gave her a snappy salute. "We'll go down to the pier," he said. "I want to show Chad what I did today."

The first stars were twinkling over the dark water as they walked out on the pier. Chad admired the neat repairs his father had made, and then they settled, side by side, with their feet dangling over the water.

"Jeannie and I found a truck in the woods," Chad told him.

"A truck!" His father was astonished. "What are you talking about?"

Chad described the narrow trail leading off the main road. "There's a clearing at the end of it," he said, "and that's where the truck is."

Mr. Weldon stood up. "I have to see that," he said. Chad knew he was smiling into the dark at the thought of some new excitement.

"I didn't know we bought a truck when we got this place," he went on. "Maybe we can put it to work."

"We can't." Chad didn't like the idea of his father going into the woods at night to see the truck. "Besides, there's something — something *funny* out there. Jeannie and I heard banging noises."

"Metal expands when it gets hot," his father said. "When it expands, it makes noises. You know that. Jeannie should know that, too." He was on his way back along the pier. "I'll just be a few minutes," he promised over his shoulder. "I'll pick up a flashlight and take a quick look at your discovery. If I don't do it now, I'll have to wait till next weekend."

Chad didn't want to stay on the pier alone, but he didn't want to go back to the clearing, either. Maybe Aunt Elsa was ready to have some boxes carried out to the pickup.

He looked out over the lake. The moon was rising, and a glittering light-path stretched across the water. It was beautiful — like a magic road leading to some mysterious place. As he watched it, something slid into the silver path, just a couple of hundred feet from the end of the pier. The dark silhouette of a rowboat danced on the surface and began to move toward shore.

Chad blinked, willing the boat to disappear. It didn't work. The empty craft drew closer every minute, and the splash of the oars grew louder.

It was coming right at him! He couldn't run away; he couldn't even breathe. Then the lonely howl of a dog echoed across the water, and the sound seemed to set him free. For the second time that day, he raced for the safety of the cabin, too frightened to look back.

Chapter Seven

"Something Bad Happened. . . ."

"Shh!"

Aunt Elsa was in the kitchen. She was standing at one side of the screen door and peering out into the moonlit backyard. Without turning around, she raised one hand and beckoned Chad to join her.

He stayed where he was. He didn't want to see what else might be out there in the night. The quicker they finished packing up and headed back to Bristol for the week, the happier he'd be.

Then he realized Aunt Elsa wouldn't just stand there at the door if she were frightened. She'd be screaming at the top of her voice. He tiptoed across the linoleum and peered over her shoulder.

"Did you ever see anything so beautiful?" she whispered.

There in the backyard, just a few feet away from the pickup, were a doe and a tiny fawn. They stood so still, they might have been statues. Only the doe's head moved, as she waited and watched.

The beam of a flashlight appeared in the road, and Chad heard the crunch of his father's footsteps. In an instant, the doe and her baby had melted away as if they had never been there.

Aunt Elsa let out her breath in a long sigh. "I'll treasure that sight," she said softly. "The world is full of wonders."

When she told Chad's father what they had seen, he gave her a hug and winked at Chad. "Maybe this isn't such a bad place after all," he said cheerfully. "Who knows what you'll see next weekend."

Chad didn't wink back. *That's the trouble*, he thought grimly. He pictured the empty boat bobbing toward him over the water. *Who knows what I'll see next weekend!*

On the drive home, Mr. Weldon talked excitedly about the truck in the woods.

"I suppose old Tim Tapper used it till it wore

out and then sold whatever parts he could," he said. "The tires are gone, and the engine. Everything's cleaned out under the hood. He could have had the whole thing towed away, but instead he hid it out in that clearing. Strange."

"Did you hear funny noises?" Chad asked cautiously.

His father shrugged. "Some. I told you, when metal heats and cools it does that."

"Tim Tapper," Aunt Elsa said. "Tim Tapper's truck. I remember something about that — but what is it?" She snapped her fingers impatiently. "It was — it was a long time ago, when I was a little girl. There was something called Tim Tapper's Tours. He was just a young fellow then. He lived in town, and he had this truck that he fixed up with benches. Took folks to Sunday School picnics and weddings and out here to the public beach sometimes. I rode in it myself once or twice. It was fun."

Chad looked at his great-aunt in surprise. She had actually known Tim Tapper. He wasn't a ghost to her; he was a real person. She had even ridden in that spooky old truck!

"But something happened." Aunt Elsa frowned, trying hard to remember. "Something bad happened, I think. People were very angry.

. . . Tim Tapper left town. . . ." She shook her head crossly. "I can't remember anymore," she complained. "That's what happens when you have too many birthdays."

Mr. Weldon laughed and changed the subject, but Chad kept thinking about what Aunt Elsa had told them. He thought about it while they unpacked the pickup, and while he was getting ready for bed, and long after the rest of the house was still.

Something very bad had happened to Tim Tapper a long time ago. What could it have been? Maybe if he knew that, he would understand the angry ghost he'd seen in the middle of the night. And maybe if he understood, he wouldn't be quite so afraid to go back to Shaky Acres.

Chapter Eight

A Sad Story

When Chad went out on the back porch the next morning, Jeannie was crouched on the bottom step fiddling with a shoelace.

"I thought you'd never come out," she complained. "I've walked up and down the alley a zillion times waiting."

"Why didn't you come in then?" Chad wanted to know. But he thought he knew the answer.

"Because your father and your great-aunt will be mad at me if they hear me asking questions about the ghost at Shaky Acres, that's why."

"What ghost?" Chad demanded grumpily.

"*You* know." She glared at him. "The one that banged on the truck when we were exploring. The one you saw — I *know* you saw him," she added, so smugly that Chad longed to smack her. "But your dad told you it was just a dream, right?"

It was no use trying to keep a secret from Jeannie. "So what?" he said. And then, because she stood there, waiting, he told her about the old man at the cabin window. And about the empty boat on the lake. And about the dog. Talking about that eerie howl gave him goosebumps.

When he had finished, he waited for Jeannie to say "I told you so," but she just stared at him.

"I think you're pretty brave," she said after a while, "for a little kid. Some kids would be screaming and yelling all over the place if that had happened to them."

It wasn't much of a compliment, but Chad decided to pretend he hadn't heard the "little kid" part. "I found out something else, too," he announced. "Aunt Elsa remembers Tim Tapper's truck. He used to give people rides in it, until something bad happened to him. She can't remember what it was, but my Grandma Weldon might know. I'm going over there now to ask her."

"I'll go, too," Jeannie said. "Okay?" Chad nodded, and they set off, stopping at the Nichols' house for Jeannie's bike.

Ten minutes later they were in Grandma Weldon's kitchen eating Oreo cookies and drinking soda.

"Of course I remember Tim," Grandma said. She grinned and pointed to the lettering on the front of her sweatshirt: IF I DON'T KNOW, NOBODY KNOWS. "Why do you ask?"

Chad and Jeannie exchanged looks. "We were just wondering what — what happened to him," Chad said. "We found his truck — "

"Oh, the truck!" Grandma Weldon clapped her hands so that all her rings flashed in the sunlight. "What fun that truck was! He called his business Tim Tapper's Tours, and you could hire him by the day. The truck was sort of like a taxi, only we didn't have real taxis in Bristol then. I remember once he drove our whole family to a Fourth of July outing. Everybody liked Tim, and he liked everybody — that was why it was so awful when he had the accident."

"What accident?" Jeannie leaned forward, almost spilling her soda.

"One December day he picked up a dozen kids to take them to a Christmas carol singing contest over in Hampton. Somehow the truck slid off the road into a field and turned over on its side. Tim got the children out before anyone else got there, but all of a sudden the whole town was in a tizzy. There was a lot of talk about how rickety the truck was. Then it turned out Tim should have had a special license to drive people around, and he didn't have one. Poor man." Grandma bit into a cookie and shook her head. "There was even an editorial in the paper about it. The town made him feel like a criminal."

"That's awful!" Chad exclaimed. "How did they know the accident was his fault?"

"Turned out it wasn't," Grandma told him. "Later the police said they'd checked the truck and it was in very good shape. Tim had been driving slow, too, but he hit an icy spot in the road, and that was that. Folks wished then that they hadn't been so quick to blame him — "

"Especially since he'd saved all their children," Jeannie interrupted. "They should have told him they were sorry."

Grandma nodded. "The trouble was, he wasn't around to hear them apologize," she said. "The day that nasty editorial appeared in the paper, he up and left Bristol. He had the property out at Perch Lake that your father bought, Chad, and he went out there to stay. Took his truck with him. They say he even lived in the truck for a while, until he built the cabin. Except for the times when he came in to pick up supplies, he never spoke to anyone in Bristol again. Acted real mean, they say. He couldn't forgive the town for turning against him without waiting to find out the truth."

"I don't blame him," Chad said. "I'd be mad at them, too." But he shivered as he remembered the fierce old face pressed up against the cabin window. Tim Tapper was still full of anger, even though he was a ghost. He didn't want the Weldons, or anyone else from Bristol, living in his cabin.

Chapter Nine

And a Terrible Night

"What time will Dad be home?" Chad asked. Friday had come again, much too quickly. He watched his great-aunt pack a carton with fresh-baked bread and cookies, a sack of potatoes, and cereal. The cooler was already filled and waiting next to the back door.

"He might be a little late," Aunt Elsa replied. "They're cutting down some trees in the town square, and they want the mess cleaned up before the weekend."

"Maybe he'll have to work tomorrow, too," Chad said hopefully. "Then we won't be able to go to the lake until tomorrow night. Or even Sunday."

Aunt Elsa looked at him. "We're going tonight," she said. "He won't change plans after I have everything packed."

Chad supposed she was right. His father had been talking about Perch Lake all week, and Aunt Elsa hadn't complained about going to the cabin the way she usually did. Since she'd seen the deer in the moonlight, she didn't seem to hate Shaky Acres so much.

I'm the only one who wants to stay home, Chad thought. A faint rumble of thunder rattled the kitchen windows, making him feel even worse. A haunted cabin in a thunderstorm — how could anybody look forward to that?

By the time his father got home, the rain was coming down hard, and they had to run back and forth to load the pickup.

"Never mind," Mr. Weldon said as he strapped a tarp over their supplies. "Rain tonight, sunshine tomorrow — that's what the weatherman says. And guess what we're going to do in the morning — we're going to fish, that's what! I borrowed a couple of rods and picked up some worms on the way home. We're all set."

Any other time, Chad would have been thrilled. He liked doing things with his father.

But all he could think about now was the long night ahead.

They got soaked all over again when they reached Shaky Acres. "You help Aunt Elsa unpack, and I'll get a fire going," Mr. Weldon said as he lit the kerosene lamps. "We'll set up our cots here in the living room tonight."

Chad was glad about that. It was bad enough to think Tim Tapper's ghost might be lurking in the dark, but it was worse when there was nothing but rusty window screens to keep him outside.

"I'll make cocoa to go with our sandwiches," Aunt Elsa said. "Cocoa's a treat on a rainy night."

She set one of the kerosene lamps in the middle of the table and, after they'd eaten, the three of them played Monopoly for an hour. Chad sat with his back to the window and tried not to hear the thunder rolling across the lake. *Maybe it would be all right,* he told himself. Maybe he'd fall asleep as soon as his head hit the pillow and not wake up until morning.

The heat from the stove and the soft lamplight made the cabin cozy. "I'm surprised the roof isn't leaking," Aunt Elsa remarked, but Chad could tell she was enjoying herself.

After a while Chad's father got out the cots and set them up close to the stove. Aunt Elsa went into her bedroom, and soon the cabin was dark except for the glow of the fire in the stove and the flashes of lightning outside.

Go to sleep! Chad ordered himself, but it never worked when you tried. Even through closed eyelids he could see the lightning, and the thunder that followed shook the cabin. He could hardly believe it when he heard his father snoring peacefully.

Gradually the lightning flashes came less often, and the thunder moved away. Chad began to think he just might fall asleep after all, when he heard a sound from the kitchen. The screen on the back door was banging. Then the doorknob rattled.

It's the wind, Chad told himself. But the rattling grew louder, and he knew he couldn't lie there waiting and wondering.

"Dad?" He kept his voice low, not wanting to wake Aunt Elsa. His father snored on.

Shivering, Chad slipped out from under the

covers. He couldn't remember where the flashlight was, so he had to feel his way through the dark to the kitchen door. *I'll open it just a crack,* he told himself, *enough to reach out and fasten the hook on the screen.*

He found the doorknob and took a deep breath. "One, two, three!" he opened the door. For one horrible second he found himself peering right into the eyes of Tim Tapper. The gray-white face was inches away from him, and one hand was reaching for the doorknob. A huge dog crowded close behind the hulking figure.

Chad was too terrified to move. He and the old man stared at each other, and then Tim Tapper and the dog vanished into the night.

Chad slammed the door and turned the lock. He raced back to his cot, stubbing his toe painfully on the way.

"What's going on out there?" Aunt Elsa called sleepily.

Mr. Weldon groaned and rolled over. "That you, boy?" he mumbled.

Chad didn't answer. His head was under the blanket and his hands were over his ears. If the screen started banging again, he wouldn't hear it. If the old man looked in through a window, he wouldn't know it. And he wasn't going to talk about what he'd seen. No one would believe him, anyway. All he wanted was to huddle right where he was and wait for the night to end.

Chapter Ten

"I Want to See the Ghost. . . ."

Chad woke to the smell of bacon and the sound of Aunt Elsa singing "Onward Christian Soldiers."

"Guess what I saw on the back porch this morning!" she exclaimed, when he staggered out into the kitchen still half-asleep.

Chad stared in horror at the open back door, remembering what *he* had seen there.

"A raccoon!" Aunt Elsa continued happily. "A big raccoon right there on the top step! He looked in at me, and I looked out at him, and then he just waddled away, calm as you please. I think he was letting me know he'd enjoy a snack once in a while." She gave Chad a gentle push. "You go and get dressed," she ordered. "Your dad's already fishing on the pier. As soon as you're ready, you can call him in for breakfast."

Chad pulled on shorts and a T-shirt and hurried down to the lake. The water glittered in the sunlight.

"No fish yet," his father reported. "But I have the feeling one's waiting for me. He's right about" — he swung his rod and sent the line a short way out across the water — "right about there!"

At once, the line went taut and the rod bent. "Ho-ho!" Mr. Weldon roared. "Got him! A nice one, too!" He gave the line a jerk and reeled in a good-sized bass.

"Wow!" Chad looked down at the fish flip-flopping on the pier. The sight of it drove thoughts of Tim Tapper right out of his head. He could hardly wait to get breakfast over with so he could start fishing, too.

Mr. Weldon's first fish was the biggest one either of them caught all morning, but they had a great time, anyway. When Jeannie's father dropped her off early in the afternoon, there was a pan full of fish cleaned and ready to fry for dinner that night.

"I'm going to start saving for my own fishing rod," Chad told Jeannie excitedly. "And my dad says someday we're going to get a boat."

Jeannie settled down at the end of the pier and tested the water with her big toe. "*If* you stay here that long," she said, looking at him sideways. "What if Tim Tapper comes back?"

"He already did." The words were out before Chad could stop them. He'd managed to forget about the ghost all morning, and he didn't want to think about him now.

Jeannie sat up straight. "What happened?" she demanded. "Come on, tell me. Did you see him last night?"

Chad sighed and told her about the old man and his dog at the kitchen door. The more he talked, the worse he felt. "But maybe it didn't even happen," he finished up shakily. "Maybe my dad's right, and I'm just having a whole bunch of bad dreams." Sitting there in the sunshine, he could almost, but not quite, make himself believe that was true.

"Oh, you saw him, all right," Jeannie said. "And you're the only person I know who's actually seen a ghost. I've been to Disneyland and I've had my ears pierced and I have a cousin who was in a movie, but I've never seen a ghost, for pete's sake."

Abruptly, she slid off the end of the pier, and

Chad jumped into the water after her. They swam and played water ball all afternoon, with no more talk about ghosts and haunting. Still, Chad could tell Jeannie had something on her mind. When they finally climbed back on the pier, panting and tired, he found out what it was.

"I want to see the ghost, too," she announced.

"What?" Chad wondered if he'd heard her right. "I thought you hated ghosts."

"I do," Jeannie insisted. "But I want to see one. And this is probably the only chance I'll ever have. Let's dry off and go out to the truck again. Maybe Tim Tapper will be there. Why should you have all the fun?"

"Fun!" Chad repeated. "That's crazy." But he could tell from the look on Jeannie's face that she'd already made up her mind.

When they went up to the cabin, Aunt Elsa had lemonade and cookies and popcorn waiting for them, so it was nearly five o'clock before they crossed the backyard and stared up the road.

"This is the dumbest thing I ever heard of," Chad muttered.

Jeannie kept walking. She didn't stop till they

reached the narrow trail branching off into the woods.

"Are you sure this is it?" she asked uncertainly. "It looks different."

Chad groaned. " 'Course this is it. It looks darker because it's so late."

For a minute he considered telling her that if she really wanted to go ghost-hunting she could do it by herself, and he'd wait for her. *Serve her right,* he thought. But he knew he couldn't let her go to the clearing alone.

"Well, come on then," he grumbled. "If we're going to the truck, let's not wait until it's really dark." He plunged into the trail and looked back over his shoulder at Jeannie to make sure she was coming. She was very pale.

She wants to turn back as much as I do, he thought. But she wouldn't admit it — not in a million years.

Chapter Eleven

"Tim Tapper's Getting Angrier. . . ."

The truck was hunkered down like a big animal in the middle of the clearing. One long spike of sun lay along the roof like a spotlight.

"I don't see anything . . . spooky," Jeannie said after a moment. Her voice sounded loud in the quiet woods. "Do you?"

Chad shook his head.

"I dare you to get in and sit in the driver's seat," Jeannie said. "I bet you're scared."

"I am not," Chad said, but he didn't move. "Why don't *you* do it? You're the one who wants to see a ghost."

Jeannie clenched her fists. "Well — " she said, and then to Chad's amazement she ran across the clearing, opened the passenger door, and climbed inside.

"Look," she shouted. "I'm driving! Who's afraid!"

Chad blinked. It seemed to him that the clearing had suddenly grown darker. "Jeannie, come on!" he shouted. But his words were drowned out by the clanking of metal against metal. The truck began to rock, just a little at first, then faster and faster. With a squeal of terror Jeannie leaped through the open door and stumbled across the clearing. Together, she and Chad raced down the trail, never slowing till they reached the road to the cabin.

"That was *awful*!" Jeannie gasped. She caught her breath and started to run once more. "I'm never coming to Shaky Acres again!"

"That's okay with me," Chad panted. "I'd just as soon go swimming by myself."

It wasn't true, and they both knew it. They were snapping at each other because they were terrified.

Just before they reached the cabin yard they stopped again. "Don't tell my folks what happened, okay?" Chad said. "They won't believe it anyway."

"Of course they won't believe it. I was there,

and *I* don't believe it," Jeannie told him. Her teeth were chattering.

"We just have to figure out some way to make Tim Tapper go away from here," Chad said, trying to calm down. "Then everything will be okay."

A horn tooted, and the headlights of the Nichols' station wagon came into sight. Jeannie looked relieved.

"*We* don't have to figure it out," she said. "*You* do. And you'd better do it fast, because I think that Tim Tapper's getting angrier." She tried to laugh and couldn't. "What a stitch!" she said, and then she ran to meet the station wagon as if she couldn't get away fast enough.

That night Chad pulled his blanket over his head as soon as his father turned out the kerosene lamp. He had to think, and he couldn't do it if he was watching the windows for a gray, scowling face and listening for the rattling of a door.

There had to be a way to make Tim Tapper leave Shaky Acres. *He's haunting us because he's angry*, Chad thought, *and he's angry about something that happened a long time ago. He hates Bristol and so he hates us, too.*

Nothing could change that, could it? Most of the town's citizens had long since forgotten all about the old man and his truck. There was no reason for them to remember unless . . . unless. . . . He drifted off to sleep.

When he woke the next morning and pushed the blanket away from his face, his father was grinning down at him.

"You look like a mummy," he said. "How can you sleep wrapped up like that?"

"I slept okay," Chad told him. "I feel great." He rubbed his eyes and realized it was true. He hadn't heard or seen a single scary thing all night but, best of all, he thought he'd found an answer to his problem.

Chapter Twelve

Chad's Great Idea

Chad explained his great idea to his father and Aunt Elsa at breakfast. He started by telling them what Grandma Weldon had remembered about Tim Tapper's accident.

"The people in Bristol were really mean to Tim," he said. "That's why he moved here and built this cabin. By the time they figured out he was really a hero for saving all their kids, he was so angry he wouldn't talk to any of them."

"Poor man," Aunt Elsa said. "He should have had a statue in his memory. Still, I don't see what you're so excited about, Chad. There's nothing to be done about all that now."

"Yes, there is!" Chad exclaimed. "I thought

of it last night. Tim Tapper loved his truck so much he never got rid of it, even after it stopped running. So what if we cleaned it up and had it hauled back to town? It could be in a playground in a park, and kids could pretend to drive it and take make-believe trips. The newspaper could remind people who Tim Tapper was, and everyone who played in the truck would honor him. The truck would be better than a statue because it would be fun!"

He looked anxiously at his father. If his father got excited about the plan, he could make it happen. He worked in the town parks, and he would know whom to ask about moving the truck.

"You've been thinking a lot about old Tapper, haven't you?" Mr. Welden said thoughtfully.

Chad nodded. He didn't want to say he'd actually seen Tim Tapper's ghost, but his father seemed to understand how important this was.

"Can we do it, Dad?" Chad asked anxiously.

His father reached over and slapped him on the back. "We'll sure give it a try," he said. "Of course, it'll take money, and the Weldons are fresh out of that! But I'll talk to the folks on the Park Board, boy. If they like your idea, maybe they'll pay for the paint and the hauling."

Every night that week Chad waited at the door as his father came home from work. Finally, on Thursday, Mr. Weldon drove into the yard with a broad grin on his face. He made a thumbs-up gesture as he climbed out of the pickup.

"The Park Board thinks my kid has a great imagination," he said proudly. "They'll pay for everything, as long as we do the work. They'll even put some old tires on the truck, after it's been moved to the park. I'm going to take part of my vacation next week so we can fix it up right away."

"What's the big hurry?" Aunt Elsa wanted to know, but Chad's father just laughed. Once again Chad had the feeling that his dad understood more than he let on.

After supper that night, the Weldons went to the hardware store to buy rust-remover and paint. When they got home, Jeannie was waiting on the back porch. It was the first time Chad had seen her all week.

She looked at their packages suspiciously. "What's happening?" she wanted to know, when Mr. Weldon had carried the supplies indoors.

Chad didn't want to tell her, but he knew she'd find out about the plan sooner or later.

As he'd expected, she thought fixing up the truck was a stupid idea. "How do you know Tim Tapper won't be mad at you for messing with his old truck?" she demanded. "How do you know he *wants* to make up with the people in Bristol?"

"He won't be mad," Chad protested. But, as usual, Jeannie had made him unsure of himself. Maybe she was right.

Maybe, when all the work was finished, he'd find that he had just made things worse.

Chapter Thirteen

Hard Work for Everybody

Chad's father had to work late again that Friday afternoon, so they decided to wait until Saturday morning to drive out to the cabin.

"All this fuss about an old truck," Aunt Elsa grumbled when they were finally on their way. "You fellows can do what you want, but I'm going to sit on the pier today and watch for herons. Mrs. Nichols told me she's seen lots of them at their place."

Later, Mr. Weldon chuckled as he and Chad trudged along the road to the clearing. "You just watch," he said. "Aunt Elsa's going to want to see what we're up to. Before you know it, she'll be checking on us."

Chad looked around uneasily, wondering who else would be checking on them. He remembered Jeannie's words — *How do you know Tim Tapper won't be mad at you for messing with his old truck?* If the ghost saw the Weldons coming into the clearing with tools and paint, he might fly into a terrible rage.

By the time they reached the truck, Chad was wishing he'd never had his great idea. His father, on the other hand, acted more excited than ever.

"We'll work on the rusty places first," he declared. He tossed Chad a piece of sandpaper. "You start on this side, and I'll work on the other."

The clearing was hot, and quiet except for the twittering of the birds. After a while Chad stopped looking over his shoulder and thought only about what he was doing. An hour passed with no sign of Tim Tapper or his dog.

The work was hard. Chad's shirt was soon soaked, and his arms ached. He was glad when he looked up and saw his great-aunt entering the clearing. She had a gallon thermos in one hand and a picnic basket in the other.

"You'd better stop and eat before you drop," she ordered. "I have enough lemonade to last all afternoon."

The three of them sat on the ground beside

the truck and ate sandwiches and chocolate cake until they were stuffed.

"I thought Jeannie might decide to come over and help," Mr. Weldon said. "She usually likes to be in the middle of things, doesn't she?"

"She says fixing up the truck is a dumb idea," Chad told him uncomfortably.

"Well, I think she's wrong," Mr. Weldon said. He finished his third glass of lemonade and stood up to stretch. "What do you say we get back to work?"

Aunt Elsa opened the truck door and peered inside. "I'm going back to the cabin for some soap and water and a scrubbing brush," she announced. "It's no good painting the outside of this machine if the inside is filthy."

Chad went with her to help carry the water buckets, and for the rest of the afternoon they all worked together, stopping only to go back to the pump for more water. By late afternoon the first coat of paint glowed in the sun, and the inside of the truck was spotless.

"Nobody's kids are going to get dirty playing in there if I have anything to say about it," Aunt Elsa told them proudly.

It was nearly five when they finished for the day and gathered up their pails and buckets.

Chad paused to admire what they'd done before he followed his family down the trail. The truck looked about a million times better, but he still didn't know whether to be pleased or worried. *How do you know Tim Tapper won't be mad . . . ?* he asked himself again. After the truck was hauled off to the town park, it would be too late to decide they'd made a mistake.

That night they went to bed early, and Chad fell asleep the minute he lay down. If Tim Tapper peered in at the window and the dog howled, he didn't know it. In the morning his arms and shoulders ached, and he noticed that his father and Aunt Elsa moved more slowly than usual. No one complained, however, and soon after breakfast they headed back to the clearing.

"You don't have to do this, you know," Mr. Weldon told Aunt Elsa. "What about those herons?"

She sniffed. "There'll be time for birds later," she snapped. "After we get this old wreck out of our woods."

The second coat of bright-red paint was completed before lunch, and by late afternoon it was dry enough for Mr. Weldon to start the lettering on the sides. Chad and Aunt Elsa watched as he measured and inked the letters, then filled them in with yellow paint.

"Tim Tapper's Tours — The Very Best," Aunt Elsa read aloud. "Well, if you like bouncing around in a truck, I s'pose that was true. I remember thinking it was a lot more fun than a regular car."

"The kids in town are going to love it," said a deep voice. "You folks are doing a fine thing."

Chad jumped, and his father almost smeared the letter he was working on. They turned to see Mr. Nichols watching them. Jeannie was behind him, looking grim.

"I wonder if Mrs. Nichols and I can ask a big favor," Jeannie's father went on. "My wife's sister has two kids down with strep throat, and she doesn't feel so good herself. We're going back to town to pick up her baby and keep him till they feel better, but we don't want to take a chance on Jeannie picking up the infection — "

"So you'd like her to stay with us for a few days," Aunt Elsa finished his sentence. " 'Course she can. We'd be glad to have her."

"I wouldn't get sick," Jeannie muttered. "I don't need to stay here."

Chad looked down at his feet. He was sorry

for Jeannie. She sounded cross, but he knew that was because she was scared. After what had happened on her last visit, she hadn't wanted to come back. Now she was trapped.

"We can go swimming before supper," he offered. "If you want to."

She shrugged. He wished he could tell her Shaky Acres wasn't haunted anymore, but of course he couldn't. He didn't know that himself.

Chapter Fourteen

One Way to Find Out

"I dare you!" Jeannie whispered. "You're still scared!" She and Chad were playing Monopoly at the living-room table. The grown-ups had settled out on the porch to enjoy the moonlight.

"Forget it!" Chad glared at her.

"If you really believed you were making Tim Tapper's ghost happy, you wouldn't be scared at all," she persisted. "You'd go out to the truck by yourself and get in it, and you wouldn't worry a bit."

"I said, forget it." For the hundredth time, Chad wished Mr. and Mrs. Nichols had taken Jeannie back to town with them. He could have told them she was too mean to get sick!

Still, he knew why she was nagging. Last weekend she'd been as frightened as Chad was

when the truck began rocking — maybe more
so. She'd raced to her parents' station wagon
and ridden away in a panic. That was bothering
her, especially since this week everyone —
even her own father — was acting as if the
truck was really neat.

"I bet you sleep with your blanket over your
head," she taunted. "I bet you wouldn't go near
that old truck unless your daddy went with
you."

Chad pushed the Monopoly board away and
stalked out to the porch. "Can we put up the
cots pretty soon?" he asked. "I'm tired."

"I should think you would be!" Aunt Elsa
exclaimed. "We all need a good night's rest."

Mr. Weldon stood up. "We'll put a cot in the
living room for Jeannie," he decided. "I'll use
my old sleeping bag out here on the porch with
you, Chad."

An hour later the cabin was quiet, but Chad
was still wide awake. He was annoyed at Jeannie, but that wasn't what kept him from sleeping. The trouble was, he knew she might be
right about Tim Tapper's ghost. Chad didn't
know that fixing up the truck was going to
make the ghost stop hating the Weldons and
everyone else who lived in Bristol. There was

one way he might find out, he supposed, and that was the thoroughly unpleasant way Jeannie had suggested. He could go out to the truck alone and see if the ghost tried to scare him away.

He got all tangled up in the sheets, just thinking about it. Finally, he kicked off the covers and pulled on his shorts and sneakers. On tiptoe, he made his way through the living room, past Jeannie's cot, to the kitchen. The big electric lantern was on a shelf close to the back door. It would give him a lot more light than the flashlight.

The door creaked as he eased it open, and he held his breath. The ghost could be just a few inches away, on the porch, or he could be prowling around out in the yard.

"See anything?"

Chad whirled around to find Jeannie right behind him.

" 'Course not," he whispered. "Go back to bed."

"What are *you* going to do?" Jeannie wanted to know. "Are you going out to the truck?"

"None of your business."

Jeannie grabbed his arm. Her face was ghost-pale in the lantern light. "You don't have to go," she said. "I was just teasing, honest. Something awful could happen to you."

Chad shook off her hand and pushed open the door. He was down the porch steps and starting across the yard before he realized she was still behind him.

"Come on back in the cabin," she begged. "Please!"

Chad thought it over. Jeannie knew now that he was no coward. She wouldn't make fun of him again. But he kept on walking. He had a peculiar feeling that he wouldn't be able to turn back, even if he'd tried. He had to go out to the clearing.

"You said I was afraid to go," he said stubbornly. "But I'm not. I'm going."

Jeannie groaned. "Then I s'pose I'll have to come with you," she complained. "Even if it's the weirdest, stupidest thing I've ever done in my life!"

Chapter Fifteen

Kidnapped!

The electric lantern made a silvery circle of light in the road. Every time Chad swatted a mosquito, the circle bounced from side to side.

The walk to the clearing seemed much longer in the middle of the night. *What if the light burns out?* Chad shuddered. The idea was too scary to think about. When they finally saw the truck ahead of them, gleaming in the moonlight, it reminded him once again of a big animal, crouched and waiting.

"See?" he whispered shakily. "There's no ghost around here. He's gone!"

"How do you know for sure?" Jeannie whispered back. "He might be inside the truck just waiting to jump out at us."

"He's not," Chad muttered, but he had to prove it. "Come on."

He held the lantern high and crossed the clearing. Jeannie followed. Together they peered in at the empty driver's seat. Gritting his teeth, Chad opened the door and looked inside. The benches along the sides of the truck were empty, too.

"I told you so," he said over his shoulder. "No ghost!" He climbed boldly into the truck and sat on one of the benches. Jeannie came after him. Hardly breathing, they listened to the buzzing of insects and the small rustling noises in the woods.

"I told you so," Chad repeated. "Tim Tapper is — "

Jeannie clutched his shoulder. "Look!" She pointed at the open front door.

Chad swung the lantern forward, just as a bony white hand clutched the door frame. Then a dark figure filled the opening. With a sound-less motion it lurched into the truck and into the driver's seat. Behind it came the shadowy bulk of a huge dog.

"Let's go!" Chad croaked. But his legs wouldn't move. Jeannie's fingers pressed painfully into his shoulder as the figure in the driver's seat reached over and closed the door. Then, incredibly, the clearing was flooded with light.

"He's turned on the headlights!" Jeannie squeaked.

It was impossible. The truck had no headlights. *I'm dreaming*, Chad told himself. *In a minute I'll wake up. . . .*

But even as he thought it, there was a rumbling under his feet. The truck — with no engine — was starting to move!

For a moment it rocked gently in place, and then it turned slowly toward the opening in the clearing. Soon it was gliding down the narrow trail and onto the wider road that led to the highway.

"No b-bumps," Jeannie stammered. Chad knew what she was thinking. Without a motor and without tires, the truck was moving smoothly over the rutted road.

Cautiously, he edged back toward the window in the rear of the truck. "I think — I think we're floating!" he exclaimed.

Jeannie slid along the bench and peeked over his shoulder. They were on the highway now, or rather they were a few feet above it.

Together they watched the road unwind below them like a dark ribbon.

Chad wondered again if he was dreaming. He closed his eyes, but when he opened them he was still in the truck.

"Tim Tapper's kidnapping us!" Jeannie wailed. "What are we going to do!" For once, it seemed, she didn't have any bright ideas.

Chad didn't have any, either. The miles flew by, and the first houses of Bristol came into sight. Their dark windows looked blank and unfriendly. Then the truck turned right, edging into a narrow street that led to Riverside Park.

"I bet he's going to the playground where the truck will be when they bring it into town," Chad whispered. "My dad said they're going to park it next to the swings."

The truck sailed through the open gates of the park. It rolled across the lawn, past the sandboxes, the teeter-totters, and the swings. Then it stopped. The driver and his dog stared straight ahead.

"What — what're they looking at?" Jeannie whispered when she couldn't bear the silence any longer.

Chad stood up. His knees felt wobbly. He took a couple of steps forward and squinted between the driver and his dog. Then he moved back hastily.

"There's a sign out there," he said hoarsely. "Right where the truck will be. It says, 'In memory of Timothy Tapper, a friend of the children of Bristol, and a hero.' That's great, huh?" The sign made him so proud that for a moment he forgot to be afraid.

"Oh," Jeannie said. She didn't speak again, even when the motor began to rumble once more and the truck backed across the lawn. Down the street they floated and out to the highway.

"We're going back," Chad said. "It's going to be okay."

Jeannie nodded. They watched the town disappear behind them and the woods close in. Soon they were gliding along the road toward the cabin, then turning onto the trail that led to the clearing. When the motor stopped, stillness closed around them like a blanket. Even the insects were silent.

"What happens now?" Jeannie whispered.

They didn't have to wait long to find out. For a moment, the two figures at the front of the truck didn't move. Then the driver turned a little, his face a gray patch in the dark. He opened the door, raised an arm in farewell, and stepped out of the truck. The dog followed, and the door creaked shut behind them.

Chad sighed. "They're gone," he whispered. "They're really gone. Forever."

He knew he was right, and for once Jeannie didn't argue.

Chapter Sixteen

Two People, One Dream

"You two are mighty quiet," Chad's father commented. "Just excited, right?"

Chad and Jeannie were squeezed like sardines between Mr. Weldon and Aunt Elsa. All four of them had been staring at the flatbed truck on the highway ahead of them. It was carrying Tim Tapper's truck to town.

Chad squirmed. "I was thinking about a really weird dream I had last night," he said, glancing at Jeannie out of the corner of his eye. "I dreamed I went for a ride in Tim Tapper's truck."

"Me, too," Jeannie said in a small voice. "I dreamed the very same thing."

"Two people, one dream." Mr. Weldon nodded. "That's unusual, but it just proves we're all thinking about the same thing."

"*I'm* thinking about getting back to the cabin to bird-watch," Aunt Elsa said briskly. "Fixing up that truck was a good thing to do, but I'm glad the job is finished. There are more enjoyable things to do at a lake cabin."

"Did I tell you the town's going to put up a sign next to the truck in honor of Tim Tapper?" Chad's father asked. "I like that."

Chad felt Jeannie's elbow dig into his side. "The sign is already — " he began, and then he stopped. *Two people, one dream*, he reminded himself. That's all it had been.

This morning the bright-red truck had been resting in the clearing exactly where they'd left it when they finished work yesterday afternoon. He and Jeannie had walked all around it while the flatbed truck was backing into the clearing. They had looked at the empty places where the headlights should have been. They had lifted the hood, just enough to see if there could possibly be a motor under it. There wasn't.

The ride in the truck couldn't have happened.

Who cares? Chad thought. *Even if it was just a dream. I think Tim Tapper was letting us know he's happy now. He doesn't hate us anymore.*

The little procession reached town and turned down the street toward Riverside Park. No one spoke as the flatbed truck turned onto the grass and trundled toward the playground. Mr. Weldon stayed close behind.

"Oh, look at that!" Aunt Elsa exclaimed suddenly. "Isn't that lovely!" She leaned so far forward that Chad and Jeannie couldn't see around her. A moment later, though, they knew what she was admiring.

"It's the sign," she said happily. "It's already there. 'In memory of Timothy Tapper, a friend of the children of Bristol, and a hero.' Now, isn't that nice! How pleased the old man would be," she went on. "I *wish* he could have seen it himself."

Chad and Jeannie looked at each other.

"I bet he would have really liked it," Chad said.

"What a stitch!" Jeannie murmured. But she wasn't laughing.

About the Author

BETTY REN WRIGHT has been scaring and delighting young readers for many years. Her books include *A Ghost in the House, The Ghosts of Mercy Manor, Christina's Ghost, Ghosts Beneath Our Feet,* and *The Dollhouse Murders.*

Ms. Wright lives in Wisconsin with her husband, George Frederiksen, who is an artist.